Contents

To Jean and Peter and Marlene and George for all their devoted work with and for children.

Charley and the Tree House

Kay Kinnear

Illustrated by Nick Ward

Scripture Union

By the same author:
Friends! Who needs them?
Muddle is my Middle Name

© Kay Kinnear 2001

First published 2001

Scripture Union, 207–209 Queensway, Bletchley, Milton
Keynes, MK2 2EB, England.

ISBN 1 85999 534 9

British Library Cataloguing-in-Publication Data.
A catalogue record of this book is available from the British
Library.

Printed and bound in Great Britain by
Creative Print and Design (Wales) Ebbw Vale.

Charley thought her new tree house
looked great. But why wasn't it higher
up the tree?

Dad explained that it had to be safe. It had to sit on a strong branch. "What will you play today?" he asked.

"Big game hunting!" cried Charley. She'd just seen it on TV. Big game hunters waited for the animals in little huts in the trees. The huts were called hides.

At that moment Jamie came round the corner of the house. He lived up the hill not far away. Jamie was in her class at school, but this was half-term.

"Brilliant!" he cried when he saw the tree house. "Let's go inside!"

Charley had bags of things ready to move in. They climbed up and down the ladder carrying them.

It took a while to get the tree house just as Charley wanted it. She took games out of a carrier bag and stacked them in a corner. She laid her cushion beside the window. Jamie put his on the other side. There wasn't any window there.

Together they spread out a tea-towel.

They put their food on it for a snack later. Gran had given Charley two small cartons of orange and two mini chocolate bars.

"Shall we hang up some pictures?" Charley asked.

"No! Let's play now," Jamie urged. "Let's play cowboys. We could be on a cliff top –"

Charley broke in, "We're not playing cowboys. We're going to play big game hunters."

Jamie didn't look pleased. "I don't want to kill animals, even pretending."

Charley laughed. "Not *shoot* animals like that, silly! Nobody wants to do that."

"I bet you didn't know taking pictures was called 'shooting'," Charley said.

"I *did* know," Jamie complained.

"You watch out of the window for animals. I'll watch out of the door."

They waited, peering round Charley's garden. It must have been at least five minutes. It seemed like hours.

All at once Charley gave a shout.

Charley snapped three pictures of the tiger. She took the last one just as its tail vanished into the bushes.

"That's Binky, our neighbour's cat," Jamie said. "She brings us mice sometimes. She scratches when you try to stroke her."

Charley nodded. "She's a proper tiger hunter."

After that tiger work, Jamie was ready for a snack.

"Shall we eat your biscuits or my mini bars," asked Charley?

"Both," Jamie answered. "I'm hungry."

"You can't have both. We have to save one for later. We'll have the mini bars," Charley said.

"Why do *you* always decide?" Jamie looked a bit cross.

"It's *my* tree house, silly."

No wild animals came by for a while. They kept watch all the time.

"I'm bored," Jamie said finally.

"Go down and be a tracker. Find something."

Jamie jumped down the ladder. He raced toward the bushes. He crawled right into them. Charley could see branches waving about. Suddenly there was lots of success all at once.

LOOK! AN EAGLE!

Charley snapped away. She got just one picture of the eagle.

LOOK! A WOLF!

But she took lots of the wolf. He looked really fierce. This was great.

Jamie was still tramping round the bushes. But soon he came back up the ladder.

"I'm tired of tracking. You track. I'll take the photos." Jamie's face looked hot. He had leaves in his hair and smudges of earth on his cheek.

"It's *my* camera. I take the photos," Charley said.

Jamie tried to grab it. Charley backed out of his way. Jamie lunged forward and caught hold of her T-shirt. They started to wrestle. Charley put the camera down behind her. Reaching round, he snatched it up.

"Hello!" It was Gran's voice from below. "Jamie's mum phoned. He's to go home for lunch now."

Chapter Two

Shark attack

After lunch, Jamie came back. The fight was forgotten. Charley suggested a new game. It was called At The Seaside. The tree house could be a lifeguard stand. A lifeguard must be on duty at all times. Below the stand, they could spread out a blue blanket. It would be the sea. They could get floating toys from the bath. Charley had thought it all out over lunch.

There's a rubber ring in the garage.

They collected the toys, the ring and the blanket. At last Charley said, "We're ready to play. I'll be the lifeguard. You be the swimmer."

"But, I want —" began Jamie.

Charley had already climbed the ladder. She was going to be a hero and save people. Afterwards, they could change places.

Jamie pretended to swim across the blanket. He made whooshing noises for splashing water. He swam and swam. He whooshed and played with the toys.

"Hurry up and get into trouble. I want to rescue you," Charley ordered from above. "Pretend to struggle."

Jamie ignored her and swam some more.

Gran called out, "Watch out for sharks!"

Jamie snapped his jaws and thrashed round on the blanket. Charley jumped down from the lifeguard stand to save the swimmer. Only there wasn't any swimmer. "I'm a shark!" shouted Jamie. "You can't grab a shark."

The shark pretended to bite Charley's leg.

Charley was cross and pushed him off. "You're not playing the game right. Anyway, *I* want to be the shark." She tried to pull Jamie off the blanket. He pretended to bite her hand. They rolled over and over on the ground.

That's enough!

"Come over to my chair, the pair of you. Sit on the grass. We'll have a little chat."

Gran looked straight at Charley. "Tell me again, Charlotte. What did you tell me you learned in your Sunday group yesterday?"

Charlotte! Charley didn't like to be called by her real name. It meant she was in trouble.

"We learned a new song," she said.

"Good, and what else?"

Charley thought for a bit. Then she remembered. "Jesus wants me to be nice to others. Like I want others to be nice to me."

"Well remembered, Charley. And are you two being nice to each other as Jesus wants?"

Charley looked at Jamie. Jamie looked at Charley.

Gran said, "That's better. And, Charley, remember to let Jamie decide your game sometimes."

Charley nodded. "OK. I'll try."

Gran got up from her chair and wiped her hand over her forehead. "It's very warm. I'll make you a cold drink. Lemon or orange?"

"Lemon!" Charley and Jamie both said together. They grinned at each other. They both wanted the same thing. Wasn't that lucky!

Gran had a surprise for them. She asked Charley to put on her swimsuit and to find a pair of shorts for Jamie. Then Gran turned on the sprinkler to water the grass. "If you want to play in the water, you can."

Of course, they wanted to.

First, the sprinkler sprayed water one way. Then it turned right round and sprayed in the other direction. Charley and Jamie danced and jumped. They twirled and ran round the water. Sometimes they were very quick. They could just miss being splashed. But sometimes…

EEEEEEEEEK! IT'S COLD!

Far too soon, Gran turned off the sprinkler. "I don't want you to get too cold," she said. She helped them dry off with a big fluffy towel.

Then it was time for Jamie to go home.

"Come again tomorrow," Charley said. They'd had such a good time. She knew they would get along fine tomorrow.

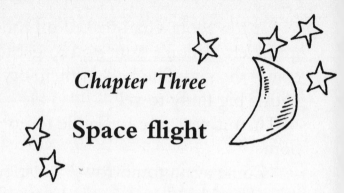

Chapter Three

Space flight

Next morning, bright and early, Jamie
knocked on Charley's door.

"Look what I've brought!" he said
proudly. It was a space helmet and belt.
On the belt was a shiny, silver space
torch. "It beams across space," Jamie
explained. "It picks out the planets."

Let's go to
the moon!

They would need lots of food for a moon journey. They'd have to eat lunch on the flight. Gran agreed. She phoned Jamie's mum and asked if he could stay till the afternoon.

Then she made a tuna sandwich and Charley made one with peanut butter and banana. Jamie cut little squares of cheese. Gran added crackers, carrot sticks, two pears and two apple drinks.

"Being an astronaut is hungry work," she said.

Charley opened up the biscuit tin. No biscuits!

Gran said, "It's amazing how fast the biscuit tin empties. I can never understand it." She smiled at Charley. "I'll bake a few fairy cakes."

Then she told Jamie, "When they're ready, you can beam them up on your torch."

They stowed the lunch in their space-packs. Charley put on her space boots.

At the bottom of the tree house ladder, Charley said, "I'll be the captain. So I'll need the helmet and belt."

"They're mine!" cried Jamie. "*I* get to wear them."

"You can't, because it's *my* moon rocket!"

"Nobody goes to the moon now!" said a voice. It was Jamie's big brother, George.

George reached out and took Jamie's helmet and belt. He said to Charley,

"You can be mission control. That's on the ground. I'll be captain and Jamie can be co-pilot."

George and Jamie climbed the ladder. Before Charley could protest, the door slammed shut. From inside the spaceship, Charley heard George shout. "START THE COUNTDOWN!"

"NO! I WON'T!" yelled Charley. "I want to be in the spaceship!"

There was no answer.

Charley raced up the ladder.

The door wouldn't open. They must be hanging on to the handle.

"You can't be ground control unless you're on the ground," George called out.

But Charley didn't want to be ground control. Or mission control. Or whatever it was. She wanted to be captain. It wasn't fair. Not fair at all. And *they* weren't being nice to her like Jesus wants. George should know about that. He was nine! She would tell Gran. She ran into the house.

Back from the moon already?

Charley dug her fists in her eyes. She wasn't going to cry. Gran would make them open the door.

Gran listened and then gave Charley a

hug. "Let them play on their own for a while. They'll let you in later. Meantime, you can help me ice the cakes."

Soon Charley was stirring cocoa and soft margarine into icing sugar. It was lovely and gooey. When the fairy cakes cooled, she spread the icing. Then, she put cherries on top. They looked scrummy. She picked out the biggest one to eat.

"George and Jamie aren't getting any cakes," she said.

Gran frowned at Charley. "What did we say yesterday? About Jesus wanting us to treat others like we want to be treated ourselves?"

"It's really hard. They're not nice to me," Charley said.

"We try anyway," said Gran.

Charley finished her cake. With a big sigh, she put the two littlest cakes on a plate. She took them outside and stared up at the tree house. It wasn't a spaceship now.

"WANT SOME CAKES?" shouted
Charley. They could at least help
themselves

Two heads popped out of the tree-
house door. Their faces looked so *smug*,
that Charley snatched up a cake and
threw it. It missed Jamie, but...

Chapter Four

Solo pilot

The boys clattered down the ladder. George tore off the space helmet and threw it on the ground. He wiped his sleeve over his face. Then he spat on his glasses and rubbed them on his jeans. Looking worried, Jamie took his cake.

"Sorry, George," Charley said. "I didn't –"

"You just wait!"

"He ate most of the lunch," Jamie muttered, "before we landed on Mars."

Would George go home now? Charley hoped so. Then she and Jamie could play Moon Journey. She could be captain like she'd planned.

George said, "C'mon, Jamie. Let's go

home and play football – not these stupid games."

Jamie looked undecided.

George picked up the helmet and grabbed Jamie's arm, "C'mon, Jamie. Space stuff is boring."

"I don't care," Charley said and stuck out her tongue at their backs. She could fly to the moon all by herself. She went into the kitchen and asked Gran for a plastic bowl. Outside she stuck it on her head. It felt like a space helmet. But it tipped whenever she moved.

Hanging on to the bowl, she climbed the ladder.

She started the countdown.

10—9—8—7—6… She got down to zero and shouted "BLAST OFF!"

She set the space ship on automatic pilot. It must be time for lunch. She opened her space pack and took out half of her peanut butter and banana sandwich. She looked out of the porthole. She checked her ship's course. Then she ate her pear and drank her juice.

It was very quiet… it wasn't much fun without Jamie.

But she might as well land on the moon. And explore! She jumped down the ladder.

The captain takes the first moon steps.

Charley took off the bowl. That was enough. This was boring alone.

She said to herself, "I'm going to play Seaside now." She spread out a blanket and pretended to be a shark. She plunged and snapped on the blanket. But there was nobody to bite. If she became a lifeguard, there was nobody to rescue.

Charley folded up the blanket. Then she had a bright idea. She could play big game hunter again. Really, she didn't need Jamie for that. She'd get her camera and wait for something to come by.

Soon she was back in the tree house. She pointed her camera at the lawn.

Almost at once she spotted something. Binky! Yesterday's tiger. But today she was only a cat. Maybe Charley could make friends with her. Binky wouldn't scratch if Charley handled her gently. Jamie and George were too rough.

Charley took her tuna half sandwich and jumped down the ladder. "Here, Binky! Here, Binky! Nice fishy."

Binky stopped and waited. She sniffed the bit of sandwich Charley held out. Then she ate it. "Good kitty," Charley said. She tore off another bit of sandwich. She put it on the bottom step of the tree house ladder. Binky ate it and jumped up another step where the next tuna bit was.

Follow my fish trail.

Binky hopped up to the last tuna piece and she was at the door of the tree house. She strolled in. Charley smiled proudly. *She* knew how to make friends with Binky much better than Jamie.

Charley thought Binky could sit on Jamie's cushion. She pushed it towards the cat. But Binky stepped round it. "Sit *there*," Charley commanded. The cat stared up with yellow-green eyes. She padded round the tree house and headed for the door.

Chapter Five

Bread and fish

Charley was really glad when Dad came home from work. She told him how everything had gone wrong in the tree house. It was all George's fault. He didn't let her be captain. He made her stay on the ground. Then he took Jamie *away!* And finally a cat bit her! She told him about Binky.

So it was terrible all day?

"Well, no," Charley remembered. "I helped Gran in the kitchen. Then we did a puzzle. I put in the most pieces! After, I watched a video."

"That doesn't sound too bad," Dad said.

Charley was puzzled. Dad didn't seem to get the point. "But the tree house didn't go right," she said again. "It's supposed to be my best thing."

"Before George came over, who was going to be captain?" Dad asked.

Charley answered slowly. "Jamie wanted to, but I —" she stopped.

"But you wouldn't let him?" suggested Dad.

Charley shook her head.

"Maybe you boss him around too much. Just like George." Dad smiled. "Poor Jamie. When does he get to be the leader?"

Dad gave Charley a hug and said, "Try sharing more. Surprising things can happen when people share."

"What sort of things?" Charley wondered.

Then Dad told her a story about sharing. It was from the Bible. Jesus was talking to a big crowd of people out in the country. When evening came, they were hungry. But there was nothing to eat.

Then Jesus' friends came to Jesus. "There's a boy here," they said, "who's got five bread rolls and two fish. But what good is that? That won't feed five thousand hungry people."

"It would be enough for the boy," said Charley. Then she thought how mean he would have felt –

"But the boy didn't eat the food by himself," Dad went on. "He thought of others and shared. He gave the bread and fish to Jesus. And Jesus blessed it."

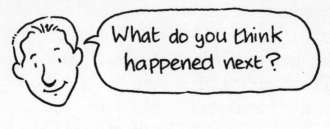

What do you think happened next?

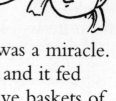

I don't know.

"What happened next was a miracle. Jesus handed out the food and it fed ALL the people. And twelve baskets of scraps were left over!"

"More than they started with!" Charley said, surprised.

Dad nodded.

"I would share my bread and fish too," Charley decided. Anyway, she didn't like fish very much. But she did like cakes a lot. She'd shared her cakes with... Then she remembered. She hadn't done that right. Oh dear, it was really hard to share. She knew Dad meant sharing more than just food things too.

Well, she would try. She jumped off the chair and said, "I've got a plan."

Dad said, "Let's hear it."

It took a little while to get just the right words for Jamie. She really wanted to be good friends again.

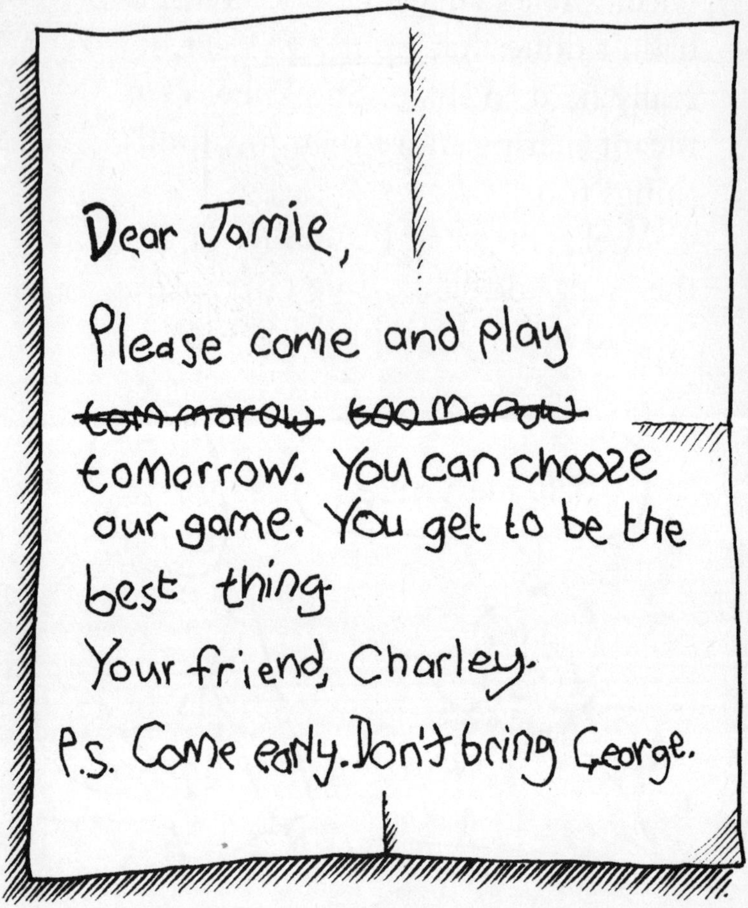

Dear Jamie,

Please come and play

~~tomorow~~ ~~too Moroo~~

tomorrow. You can chooze
our game. You get to be the
best thing

Your friend, Charley.

P.S. Come early. Don't bring George.

Charley folded up the letter. She put it in an envelope. "I hope Jamie will let me be leader sometimes."

Dad grinned. "I'm sure he will. But give him a good go first."

Charley put on a jacket. Then she and Dad walked up the hill to Jamie's house.

Chapter Six

The flood

In the middle of the night, Charley
woke up. The wind howled outside.
She could hear rain beating on the
window. But she was cosy in bed. Dad
was in the next room. God was keeping
her safe. She went back to sleep almost
at once.

In the morning the sun streamed through the window. Still sleepy, she looked out at the tree house. She hoped Jamie had planned a good game. Then she stared down. The garden was a lake! What had happened? How could they get to the tree house?

She ran downstairs in her pyjamas. "Dad, Dad," she cried, "The garden's all watery! It rained a lake!"

Dad was drinking tea and reading his newspaper. "It's not all rain," he said. "Come with me."

They went to the front door and looked out.

"It has poured water into our garden all night," Dad added. "There was all that rain too. No play in the tree house today, I'm afraid."

But Charley had another idea.

We could play Noah's Ark. I'll be Noah.

She told Dad about the story Gran had read to her. There was lots of rain and a Big Flood. God helped a man called Noah to build a large boat. It was called an Ark. So, Noah, his family, and all kinds of animals were saved.

Dad said he knew the story and that she'd told it well. Then he asked, "Aren't you forgetting something?"

Charley remembered. Jamie! Jamie's game. Well, they could play *that* any time. They must play Big Flood today! She would have to be Noah. After all, she knew the story. She explained this to Dad.

"Charlotte!"

Charlotte! Not Charley. Uh-oh!

"You've written to Jamie that it's his choice today," Dad pointed out. "You can't play in the garden anyway. It's not safe and clean until the water has drained away."

Charley was disappointed. They couldn't play Noah's Ark. Now Dad was disappointed with her too. She'd forgotten about sharing already. Next, she would have to disappoint Jamie.

No tree house today, Jamie. There's a lake.

Brilliant! Can I see it?

43

Jamie wasn't sad at all. He wanted to come over right after breakfast. Afterwards, they could play at his house. Charley's dad took the phone then and spoke to Jamie's mum. Yes, it was all right to spend the morning there.

Charley cheered up. Maybe it would be a good day after all.

Dad left for work. Charley helped Gran cook their breakfast. Gran boiled two eggs. Charley buttered brown toast. To finish, Gran cut toast soldiers.

Charley told Gran about how she was trying to share with Jamie. Dad had been talking about sharing. Gran smiled. "Sharing is part of always being kind to others. So we've talked about it too."

Charley chewed her last toast soldier. Then she said, "It's so hard to remember. Don't *you* think so?"

Gran agreed it wasn't always easy. She smiled. "But you can pray. You can ask Jesus to help you keep trying."

Just then the doorbell rang. It was Jamie. He thought the lake was great.

He watched the water company men working. Then, he and Charley walked up the hill to his house. Gran stood on the pavement and watched them go. They turned round and waved goodbye when they reached Jamie's house.

"Mum says the sun has dried the grass. We can play in our tent."

Jamie and his mum carried a canvas bag out of their garage.

Finally the tent was all set up. Charley started to say, "I want to pl..." Then she stopped. It was Jamie's choice today.

"What are we going to play?" she asked.

"Let's play Red Indians." He pointed to the tent. "This is our tepee. We can take my bow and arrow. We'll go hunting, then –"

I'll be the Indian chief.

Chapter Seven

On the trail

Here was George again! Charley was worried. What if he tried to get even about the cake? Anyway, he always took over and had to be the leader. Maybe he wouldn't let her play. And today was supposed to be Jamie's day.

Charley spoke up. "It Jamie's turn to be leader, I mean, chief."

"Who says?" demanded George.

"I say!" said Charley.

I'm bigger.
I'm older.
It's my house.

But...

Let's just play.

Then George told them he had a plan. "Pretend you're Red Indian braves. I'm the chief. I'll train you to be trackers. You can follow my trail." He turned to Jamie. "Go and get our old Indian headbands."

Charley wanted to object. She didn't want to play with George. But this sounded like fun. She would wait and see.

Jamie came back with two stretchy headbands. Each had four feathers and a broken one.

"You can wear mine," George said, waving his hand at Charley. "It's too small for me, anyway."

But it was just right for Charley.

George had fetched a blanket from their garage. He wrapped it round his shoulders. He pointed at the tent.

"Sit, Braves. Shut eyes and count to hundred. Then, Braves, follow trail."

At last they reached one hundred.
They crawled out of the tent. At first
they couldn't see any trail to follow.
Then Jamie spotted the first sign.

"Look!" he cried.

Now, Charley knew what to search for. She found the second arrow.

It pointed towards a prickly bush. Would their chief mark a trail through it? They hoped not. They kept looking. Charley peered into the grass. Jamie hunted on the other side of the bush. Then, they spied the arrow together!

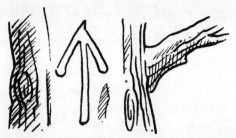

"Does he mean we have to climb the tree?" Charley asked.

"I don't know, " replied Jamie. "There's no ladder like your tree house."

They stared up into the tree. Then they saw it.

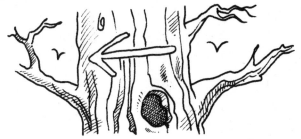

"*He* climbed the tree!" cried Charley in surprise.

"He's always doing that," said Jamie. "Mum tells him not to. He broke his arm once."

The top arrow pointed at the fence. They explored along it. They didn't know whether to look for chalk marks or sticks or stones.

Charley said suddenly, "We should have Red Indian names."

I'll be Great Arrow.

I'll be Running Deer.

They came to a gate. Low down on the gate was a tiny arrow. It pointed into the next garden.

"Can we go into your neighbours' garden?" Great Arrow asked.

"It's OK." Running Deer pushed the gate open.

The grass was long and tufty. There were lots of large bushy plants and tall trees, perfect for tracking. They searched around for the next mark

Suddenly from behind one of the trees…

"Hi Grandad," Running Deer said, shoving away Great Arrow.

Grandad! Great Arrow felt silly. She'd forgotten that Jamie's grandad and nan lived next door.

"We're Red Indian Braves following a trail," Running Deer explained.

"Oh, so that's what George was doing," Grandad said. "I saw him from the window and came out to see." He pointed, "I think, Braves, that's your next marker."

The arrow was made out of holly berries. The berries weren't bright red now. They were all dried up and black.

"What will we find at the end of the trail?" Great Arrow asked.

"George, I suppose," replied Running Deer.

"I don't want to find George."

"Nor me."

The two Braves giggled. Tracking was fun, even if it only led to George.

The next three markers they found quickly.

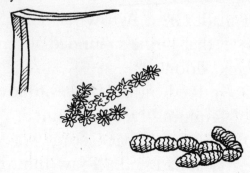

The last arrow led them to the gate again and into Running Deer's garden. Great Arrow spotted a stick arrow by the back fence near a pile of leaves. The Braves must be getting near the trail's end. Maybe there was a prize. She raced towards the arrow and…

Ha! Ha! Ha! You found my animal pit!

Great Arrow climbed out of the hole. She brushed off leaves and earth. What a pest George was! This was because of the cake she had thrown at him.

"OK," she said to George. "Brave make peace with Chief." She put up her hand like a Red Indian.

He slapped high fives, not like a Red Indian. But he said "Peace!" and pointed at the tepee. "Faithful Braves! Search in tepee for trackers' reward."

Great Arrow and Running Deer found two small peanut crisp bars. They sat down to eat them.

"I didn't like your bossy brother's trap," said Great Arrow. "But I liked the rest of his trail."

Running Deer's mouth was too full to answer.

Chapter Eight

Two by two

After lunch Gran told Charley the good news. She could play in the tree house. "The water has drained away. The ground is soggy, so wear your wellies."

Charley phoned up Jamie. She asked if he would like to play Noah's Ark. "It's supposed to be your choice today," she said. When he agreed with the idea, Charley told him what to bring.

My animals and George's and my big sister's too.

"The animals should be in twos," said Charley. "One girl and one boy. That's how they went into the Ark."

Both Charley and Jamie owned a rabbit. Two rabbits. There were two cats and two dogs too. Charley had a lion and Jamie, a tiger.

"They're nearly the same," said Jamie.

One problem was far too many teddies.

"We can't have them all," said Charley.

"Why not?" asked Gran, who had come into the lounge. "There are all kinds of bears. Brown bears, black bears, grizzly bears, polar bears, and many more."

What people went into the Ark besides Noah?" asked Jamie. He couldn't remember all of the story.

Charley knew. "There was Noah's wife. Then he had three sons. And they had wives."

"I get to be Noah," said Jamie.

"But you—but I—but–" Charley stopped. She longed to say, but *I* know the story better. It's *my* tree house. *I* should be Noah. Then she remembered what Dad had said. She must share.

"OK," she said. She gave only a very little sigh.

"You can be Noah's wife," Jamie offered. "That must be next best."

"She doesn't do anything in the story," Charley said. "I'll be a giraffe girl."

They put on their wellies and took the animals outside.

They arranged all the animals and shut the door.

Charley said, "Then, it rained for forty days and forty nights." They looked out of the Ark window. The window was streaky so it looked like rain.

Gran had packed a snack for their time in the Ark. But first they fed the animals bits of bread.

They ate their snack. It was apples
and muesli bars. There was a carton of
orange juice each. Charley had stopped
being a giraffe. She decided, after all, to
be Mrs Noah. She had to be able to
talk.

They bedded down the animals.
They pretended to sleep.

"Let's count to forty," suggested Charley.

"We should count twice," said Jamie. "You do the days. I'll do the nights."

"OK." Charley thought that was a good idea.

Soon forty days and nights were over. They waited a while longer. The animals got more food. Then it was time for Noah to find out if the water had gone.

Charley the dove flew out from the Ark twice. The second time she brought back a green branch. This meant the land was dry again. They could leave the Ark. They started to take the animals, two by two, down the ladder.

"God sent a rainbow at the end," Charley told Jamie. "No more rain like that."

"I wish we'd see one," he said.

"Me too," said Charley. But the sun was shining brightly and that was good too. They took the animals into the house. Charley peered inside her rucksack. She saw two marshmallow biscuits inside. She hadn't noticed them before. One was squashed. One of the animals must have stood on it – probably a grizzly bear.

"I like marshmallow," said Jamie.

"Me, too," said Charley.

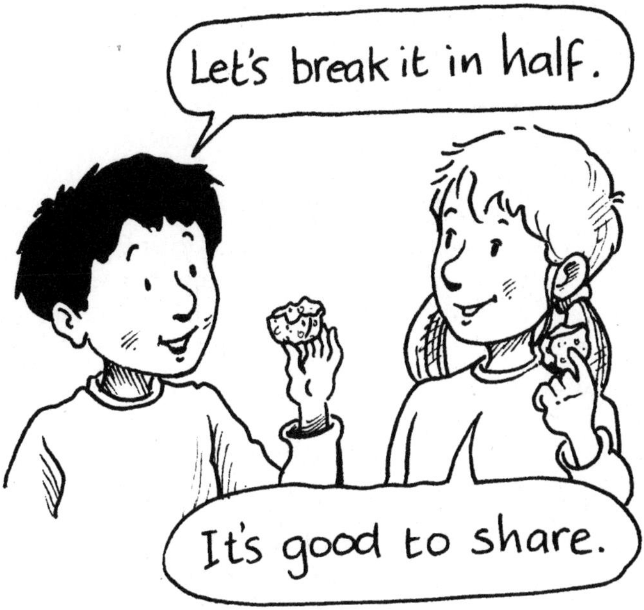
Let's break it in half.
It's good to share.

Here are some are other Roller-coaster books for you to explore:

1,2,5 Go!
Hilary Hawkes

Sounding its horn, the 125 engine was going at full speed through Jack's garden. It went round the shed and just missed the washing basket by the back door. Jack had played this game a hundred times before, usually with Richard, his best friend. But Richard has moved house and new people have moved in next door. Will this be the end of the train games?
ISBN 1 85999 439 3
Price £3.50

Tales of Young Maximus Mouse
Brian Ogden

"Do you remember that day at school when we swapped the cheese for plasticine?" asked Maximus. "Too right," said Mick. "All the mouselings and teachers picked up the plasticine and took a big bite. It was a pity they caught us though! We missed our playtimes for a week."
ISBN 1 85999 328 1
Price £3.50

Maximus Mouse and Friends
Brian Ogden

"HELP!" yelled Maximus as he hurtled down the hill on his new rollerblades. Patrick just had time to grab the new pink duvet he had bought for Paula and hold it up for Maximus to crash into. "Patrick, you're always there when I need you," gasped Maximus.
ISBN 1 85999 362 1
Price £3.50